To Sara,
my daughter, muse,
and able assistant

Published by Bloomsbury U.S.A. Children's Books, 175 Fifth Avenue, New York, New York 10010
Distributed to the trade by Macmillan

Library of Congress Cataloging-in-Publication Data
Baicker-McKee, Carol.
Mimi / Carol Baicker-McKee. — 1st U.S. ed.
p.   cm.
Summary: Mimi the pig and her bunny spend a very busy day at the library, the park, and home, but all the while she is
thinking of her pet roly-poly bug, Frank, who has been missing since breakfast.
ISBN-13: 978-1-59990-065-0 • ISBN-10: 1-59990-065-3 (hardcover)
ISBN-13: 978-1-59990-281-4 • ISBN-10: 1-59990-281-8 (reinforced)
[1. Lost and found possessions—Fiction. 2. Pets—Fiction. 3. Wood lice (Crustaceans)—Fiction. 4. Pigs—Fiction.] I. Title.
PZ7.B1436Mim 2008   [E]—dc22   2007050756

Book design by Daniel Roode
Typeset in Venetian
The art in this book is multimedia relief, constructed with fabric, illustration board, stuffing, pipe cleaners, polymer clay,
wood, wire, and the occasional mystery object from the junk drawer. No actual pigs, bunnies, or bugs were harmed in the
making of this book, although the illustrator did prick her finger badly enough to need a Band-Aid.

First U.S. Edition 2008
Printed in China
1 3 5 7 9 10 8 6 4 2 (hardcover)
1 3 5 7 9 10 8 6 4 2 (reinforced)

All papers used by Bloomsbury U.S.A. are natural, recyclable products made from wood grown in well-managed forests.
The manufacturing processes conform to the environmental regulations of the country of origin.

mimi

Carol Baicker-McKee

BLOOMSBURY
CHILDREN'S
BOOKS

Here is Mimi.

Here is Bunny.

And here is Mimi's pet,
Frank the roly-poly bug.
He lives in this special yogurt cup.

Every morning, Mimi shares a drink of milk and a bite of cereal with Bunny.

She shares a smidge of banana with Frank.

Wait, where *is* Frank?

Is he climbing up his stick? No.

How about sleeping under his rock? No.

Maybe Frank is hiding under his food? No.

Come out, Frank! Don't you want your banana smidge?

No?

"Don't worry," Mommy says.
"I'm sure Frank will turn up later.
Now go get ready for library school."

Oh! Library school!

Time for Mimi to put on her cape,

her tiara,

and her sunglasses.

Bunny likes to come too.

Frank has to stay home.

No bugs allowed at the library.

Besides, today he is missing.

Here's what Mimi does at library school:

Listens to stories.

Sings songs.

Dances a little.

Laughs a lot.

Here's what else she's supposed to do:

Wear underpants!

After library school, it's time for the park.

Mimi pushes Bunny in the swing.

Bunny doesn't like to go too high.

But Mimi does!

Then Mimi and Bunny

zip down the slide

at least a zillion times . . .

. . . and hunt for bugs. They find a caterpillar, three ants, a worm, and a snail.

But no Frank.

Mimi and Bunny have a nice nap on the way home,

but then Mimi wakes up **cranky.**

She has to blow bubbles to feel better.

Lots of bubbles.

Before dinner, Mimi sets the table.

One fork for Daddy,

one for Mommy,

one for Bunny,

and two for Mimi—because she likes forks.

No fork for Frank. He doesn't have any hands.

Plus, he is *still* missing.

When it's time to get ready for bed,

Mimi and Bunny need:

3 stories,

2 belly zerberts,

and **1** "I See the Moon" song.
Mimi hopes the moon sees Frank, wherever he is.

Then it's lights out—except for the twinkle star
night-light, of course.

Hey! Something is tickling Mimi's leg!

"Daddy! Mommy!

Monster!"

Oh, it's not a monster, it's Frank!

Mimi tucks Frank in under his food.

Then Mommy and Daddy give Mimi
another belly zerbert.

"You forgot Bunny," Mimi says.
There. One for Bunny.

"And Frank," Mimi says.

But Mommy thinks Frank is too sleepy.

Daddy and Mommy sing
the moon song once more,

while Mimi and Bunny curl up
snug and cozy . . .

. . . just like Frank.

'Night 'night, everyone.